ThunderTrucks! is published by Stone Arch Books
a Capstone imprint
1710 Roe Crest Drive
North Mankato, Minnesota 56003
www.mycapstone.com

Cataloging-in-Publication Data is available on the
Library of Congress website.

ISBN: 978-1-4965-6493-1 (hardcover)
ISBN: 978-1-4965-6497-9 (eBook pdf)

Summary: Jason is ready to win the famous golden
fender, but it's not going to be easy. He has to take
on the likes of Perseus and The Hydra in a freestyle
event. While he is doing wheelies and donuts, one evil
official is trying to make sure Jason gets crushed by
his completion.

Designed by Brann Garvey

Printed in the United States of America
PA021

THUNDERTRUCKS!

FREESTYLE FUN

BY BLAKE HOENA

ILLUSTRATED BY
FERN CANO

STONE ARCH BOOKS
a capstone imprint

CONTENTS

CHAPTER 1

THE PIT

Argonutz rolls up to The Pit. It is a large arena in the center of the capital city of Trolympia.

The front gate is open, so he drives inside.

Construction trucks rumble. They are setting up for the Freestyle Jam.

Around the top of the arena, banners
flutter in the wind. Each has an image
of a famous ThunderTruck. One shows
Atalanta, the World's Speediest Truck.
Another shows Hercules, the World's
Mightiest Truck. Argonutz also sees
banners for Perseus, Odysseus,
and Theseus.

"One day, I will have a banner up there," he whispers.

Argonutz looks around the empty stands. He imagines they are full of excited fans, beeping his name. "Argonutz! Argonutz!"

HONK! HONK! His daydream is suddenly interrupted.

"Outta the way, kid," a large dump truck honks.

"Sorry," Argonutz says. He backs up.

The dump truck rumbles past. It drops a load of dirt in the center of the arena. A bulldozer pushes the dirt into a large mound.

"You shouldn't be here, kid," the dump truck says.

"But I will be competing in the Freestyle Jam," Argonutz says.

"Sure you are," the dump truck honks.

"But I am. I'm a ThunderTruck," Argonutz says. "And I'm going to win the Golden Fenders!"

The dump truck looks from Argonutz to the banners flying above The Pit.

"Then why don't I see you up there?" he asks.

"Because I'm not famous yet," Argonutz replies as he rolls away.

"Well, nobody can beat the freestyle champ, Medea!" the dump truck shouts. "She is magical."

"But I'm agile," Argonutz mumbles.

Every ThunderTruck has a special ability. Perseus can jump farther than any truck. Theseus can outsmart other trucks.

Argonutz is super nimble. He can dart and dodge faster than anyone. He is just not sure how being agile will help him win the Freestyle Jam.

Soon, everything is ready.

"Wow!" Argonutz exclaims.

A huge tabletop stands in the middle of
The Pit. On the far end rises a rock wall.
A couple of ramps are along the right
side of the arena. On the left, junked cars
have been piled up into huge mounds. In
all four corners of the stadium are tall
sandy berms.

From above him, Argonutz hears the
rumble of excited trucks. The stands are
now full of fans.

"Hercules! Hercules!" they honk.

"Atalanta! Atalanta!" they beep.

But none cheer his name as Argonutz rolls over to the garage where the other competitors wait.

Argonutz joins famous ThunderTrucks like Theseus and Perseus. He also sees some of the worst MonsterTrucks, like Bullistic and the three Chimera Brothers.

Argonutz feels small next to the other trucks. The competition is going to be tough.

"Welcome to the Freestyle Jam!" an official blares.

The crowd goes wild, filling The Pit with loud cheers.

"ThunderTrucks and MonsterTrucks will compete for the fabulous Golden Fenders."

The crowd roars even louder.

A tall pole is mounted to the rock wall at the end of the arena. A golden fender sits on top of the pole. The fender shines in the sun.

"Many have tried to win them," the official continues. "But none have been able beat our reigning champion, Medea."

A scary truck rolls into the arena. She is surrounded in an eerie light.

The crowd goes quiet.

MonsterTrucks are mean and tough. They often cheat. But Medea is one of the creepiest trucks around. Other trucks rattle in fear whenever she drives by.

"Good luck," she honks at the other competitors as she rolls into the garage.

"The rules are simple," the official says. "First, every truck will have two minutes to do tricks and score points. The top four trucks move on to the final round to compete against Medea."

Argonutz looks up to the banners waving from the top of the arena. *I can do this,* he says to himself.

"Let the competition begin!" the official blares.

CHAPTER 2

PRELIMS

"First up, Perseus!" the official yells.

"Perseus! Perseus!" the crowd roars.

Perseus revs his engine. Then he speeds off in a cloud of dust.

He heads straight for the tabletop. He races up one side. Then he flies all the way to the other side. He is the best jumper around.

Perseus speeds around a berm. Then he heads straight up one ramp and sails all the way to second ramp.

Perseus performs trick after trick, jumping all over the place.

When he is done, a score flashes up on the big screen: 9.0. The crowd roars.

Next up is Bullistic. He speeds out of the garage and charges straight at the pile of junkers.

He plows through the mound. Bumpers, tires, and spare parts fly everywhere. Bullistic continues to spin, crushing and crashing into cars. His score is 7.2.

When it is Atalanta's turn, she zips

around the track almost too fast to see. She zooms around a berm and flies over a ramp. Around and around she races. She earns a score of 7.9.

The Goat, one of the Chimera Brothers, is up next. He rams into things and knocks over both ramps. He scores 4.7.

Hercules uses his mighty horsepower to push the ramps up. Afterward, he is exhausted, and smoke pours out of his engine. He scores 4.8.

The Lion, another Chimera Brother, tears up one of the berms with his spiked bumper. He scores 2.3.

 Theseus zigzags around the arena like he is winding through a maze. He scores 8.8.

The Dragon, the third Chimera Brother, races up the rock wall. He does a backflip while breathing fire. He scores 9.3.

After each trick, the crowd honks and

beeps excitedly.

"Next up, Argonutz!" the official shouts

through the loudspeaker.

Argonutz slowly rolls out onto the

sandy surface of The Pit.

Silence.

No one beeps or honks.

"Who's the kid?" sometruck in the crowd asks.

Argonutz revs his engine. He looks up at the banners. *I will be up there one day,* he thinks to himself.

Then spinning his tires, he takes off in a cloud of dust. He heads straight for one of the ramps and flies over it. But not as far as Perseus did.

No one cheers.

Then he zips around one of the berms. But not as fast as Atalanta did.

No one honks.

Next he races over some of the
junkers. But he does not crush them like
Bullistic did.

No one beeps.

Argonutz is about to race up the wall
and do a flip like The Dragon. But he
hears Medea laugh.

"Give it up, kid," she says.

"I'm just warming up,"
Argonutz says, frustrated.

He knows that he needs to
do something different. He cannot jump
like Perseus or crush things like Bullistic.
He is not as fast as Atalanta and cannot
breathe fire like The Dragon.

But he is quick and agile!

He races toward the tabletop. As he nears the top, he slams on his front brakes. That makes his back end flip up. He flips up onto the tabletop, landing with a *THUD!*

No one cheers.

Argonutz looks around, worried.

Did I do something wrong? he wonders.

Then he hears sometruck quietly whisper, "Did you see that backflip?"

Another trucks mumbles, "Whoa, I've never seen that trick before."

Then a little louder, a truck honks, "That was amazing."

The crowd cheers.

Argonutz looks up at the timer. He has less than a minute left. He needs to do something fancy.

Argonutz speeds toward one of the ramps. Instead of going straight up, he hits it with just his left tires.

It seems like he will flip over and crash. But as he flies up the ramp, he twirls through the air. Then he lands on all four tires. *THUD!*

He hits the second ramp. This time, he lands with just his right tires. He twirls through the air again. And lands. *THUD!*

The crowd honks and beeps. Then the buzzer sounds. His time is up.

On the scoreboard the results flash.

DRAGON	9.3
PERSEUS	9.0
THESEUS	8.8
ARGONUTZ	8.5
ATALANTA	7.9
BULLISTIC	7.2

Argonutz did it! He is moving on to the final round to face Medea.

CHAPTER 3

FREE-FOR-ALL

For the final round, the competition is a trick-for-trick challenge. Medea leads the way and does a trick. The other competitors have to follow her and match her tricks to continue on.

"Let's see what you got," Medea hisses at Argonutz. Then she enters The Pit.

Medea races up the tabletop. But instead of flying over it, she leans back as she reaches its top. This causes her to fly almost straight up. She lands in the middle of the tabletop on her back tires.

The crowd roars.

Argonutz follows. He lands a little wobbly, but he matches her trick. Theseus, Perseus, and The Dragon match the trick.

Next, Medea races toward the rock wall. Just as it looks like she is about to smash into it, she slams on her front brakes.

Her back end flips up so that she's on her front tires. Then she rolls backward for a trick called a moonwalk.

The crowd honks excitedly.

Argonutz follows her trick.

As Theseus nears the wall, he does not hit his breaks hard enough. He slams into the wall with a **KRAK!** He stumbles backward. He cannot keep going.

Then Perseus does the trick. And The Dragon.

"One down and three to go," Medea

hisses as she sails over one of the ramps.

Argonutz follows her. Then Perseus.

But as Perseus flies through the air,

The Dragon hits him with a blast of fire.

All four of his tires go ***POP!***

POPPITY! POP! POP!

Perseus lands with a ***THUD!*** and is

unable to move.

Now it's just Medea, Argonutz, and the Dragon.

Medea zips around berms, spins 360s, and rides on two tires. Both Argonutz and The Dragon match her trick for trick.

After every trick, The Dragon tries to fry Argonutz with blasts fire. Luckily, he is quick and nimble. He does trick after trick while avoiding being burned to a crisp.

"I'm done with tricks. It's time to end this," Medea hisses.

She speeds toward the mound of junkers. Just as she is about to crash into it, she flashes her lights. **BOOM!** Cars going flying up into the air.

Argonutz is not worried until they start crashing down around him. He hits his brakes **THUD!** He dodges to the right. **KRAK!** He darts to the left. **THUMP!** He speeds ahead. **WHAM!**

Argonutz dodges the falling junkers and catches up to Medea.

"Looks like it's just you and me, kid," she hisses.

Argonutz looks back. The Dragon has been buried under a pile of wrecked cars.

"I think it's time for you to lead," Medea honks. Her lights begin to shine.

"Uh-oh!"

CHAPTER 4

GOLDEN FENDERS

"If I can't beat you with my tricks,"

Medea beeps, "I will do it with my magic."

Medea blasts the ground at his tires.

BOOM! The ground explodes. Argonutz

leaps back just in time. He whips a 180

and speeds off.

He gets up on his right tires as Medea

blasts the ground beneath him again.

BOOM!

Then he gets up on his left tires. **_BOOM!_**

Argonutz leaps over a ramp as Medea blasts it apart. **_BOOM!_**

He ducks behind the other ramp, and Medea blasts it to pieces. **_BOOM!_**

The crowd squeaks and rattles with every blast. The course is covered in rubble. Argonutz zips around a berm. Medea blows it up. **_BOOM!_**

He flips over the tabletop as a blast of light sizzles by. **ZZTT!** Argonutz lands facing Medea.

"You can't escape me forever," she beeps, shining her lights at him.

Argonutz pops a wheelie as the blast
rocks the ground at his tires. **_BOOM!_** He
spins around, while still on his back tires.
Then he races off.

She's right, Argonutz thinks. He is
running out of gas. He does not know
how much longer he will last.

Ahead of him rises the rock wall. On top is the Golden Fender. He races toward it as Medea chases him. She sends blast after blast of light at him. He ducks and dodges and darts out of the way.

Then he is at the wall. The treads of his tires grab its rocky surface. He is climbing up, up, up, as fast as he can.

Medea flashes her lights and sends a blast. **KRAK!** It melts Argonutz's mud flaps. The rock wall shudders.

Medea shoots another blast. **KRAK!** It just misses his back tires. As he races up, Argonutz feels the rock wall quake and shudder.

KRAK! Another blast smashes into the wall. It starts to sway back and forth.

Argonutz guns his engine. His tires spin as he loses his grip on the wall. He flips backward, end over end.

As Argonutz starts to fall, the rock wall crumbles. Rocks **CRASH!** *BOOM!* **THUMP!** to the ground.

Argonutz flips through the air once, twice, three times as he falls.

"My axle!" he honks as he lands hard. Rocks continue to *CRASH! BOOM!* **THUMP!** in front of him.

When the dust clears, Argonutz is alone. Where is Medea?

Medea has been crushed under the rocks. The Golden Fenders are lying on the ground next to him. Even covered in dirt they shine.

"Argonutz wins!" the official blares over the loudspeaker.

The crowd goes wild, honking and beeping loudly. The other ThunderTrucks roll up to Argonutz in amazement.

"Are you hurt?" Atalanta asks.

"Let me haul you to Poly-D's," Hercules offers.

On the way to Poly-D's Repair & Salvage Shop, Argonutz repeats the story of how he beat Medea. He repeats it again and again and . . .

". . . and then the rock wall crumbled," he says for the hundredth time.

"Are we there yet?" Theseus asks.

"I can't listen to him any longer," Perseus adds.

" . . . I landed with a **KRAK**, and . . .

CHAPTER 5

FIXED UP

The ThunderTrucks wait outside
Poly-D's Repair & Salvage Shop. They are
all banged up from the FreeStyle Jam.

Perseus has four flat tires. Theseus'
front bumper is about to fall off.
Puffs of black smoke pour out from
Hercules' engines.

Inside comes the **_VRRRTTT!_** **_VRRRTTT!_** of an air wrench followed by the **CLUNK! CLUNK!** of lug nuts hitting the floor.

"Ow, ooh, my axle," Argonutz whines.

He is on a lift in the back of the garage. One of his front tires is on the floor.

"Oh, stop complaining," says Poly-D, the shop's owner. He is a rough-looking tow truck. "It's just a bad sprain."

"But it hurts so much!" Argonutz beeps.

Poly-D shakes his hood.

Again, the air wrench sounds.

VRRRTTT! VRRRTTT!

Then lugs nuts **CLUNK! CLUNK!** on the floor.

"Ow, ooh, ow," Argonutz whines again.

His other front tire falls off and rolls up to a pair of golden fenders in the corner of the garage.

"Where did you get those fenders?" Poly-D asks.

"I won them at the Freestyle Jam," Argonutz says.

"Really?" Poly-D asks.

"Yeah!" Argonutz replies. "I am agile!"

"Oh, really," Poly-D says. "Then how'd you sprain your axle?"

"Well, let me tell you—," Argonutz starts to say.

But he is interrupted by the other ThunderTrucks.

"Noooo!" Hercules groans.

"Not again!" Perseus moans.

"How many times do we have to hear that story?" Theseus complains.

"Anything is better than listening to him whine," Poly-D rumbles back at them. "Let's hear it."

Argonutz tells the entire story again.

***

". . . and that's how I sprained my axle," Argonutz finishes.

"Well, you're all fixed now," Poly-D says. "And set to go."

Argonutz has all four tires on. He also wears his golden fenders. He rolls over to a mirror and flashes his lights happily.

"These look pretty good on me," he beeps.

Then he drives out of the garage.

All the other ThunderTrucks are waiting

for him.

They hold up a banner with his image

on it.

"We thought you deserved this,"

Theseus says.

"For beating Medea," Hercules adds.

"Let's go hang it up in The Pit,"

Atalanta says.

"Okay," Argonutz beeps. "And on the

way, I can tell you the story of how I won

the Golden Fenders."

All the ThunderTrucks groan,

"Nooooooo!"

ARGONUTZ

Freestyle Fun was inspired by myths of Jason and the Argonauts. Jason was a famous Greek hero. His father was King Aeson, ruler the Greek kingdom of Iolcus.

Jason's uncle captured Aeson and took control of Iolcus. The only way for Jason to get the throne back was to find the Golden Fleece.

This magical hide was from a golden ram that once belonged to Jason's ancestors. It would give Jason the right to the kingdom.

For his quest, Jason asked for help. Famous heroes from across the land joined him. They included Hercules, the strongest person in the world, and Atalanta, the fastest person in the world.

Jason also had a mighty ship built, the Argos. The heroes that sailed with Jason were called the Argonauts.

The Golden Fleece was in Colchis, a land ruled by King Aeetes. The king did not want to give Jason the fleece. So he made Jason earn it by giving him several deadly challenges to complete. But luckily for Jason, the king's daughter, Medea, wanted to help him.

With Medea's aid, Jason retrieved the Golden Fleece. He sailed back to Iolcus and became its king.

BLAKE HOENA

Blake Hoena grew up in central Wisconsin, where he wrote stories about robots conquering the moon and trolls lumbering around the woods behind his parents' house. He now lives in St. Paul, Minnesota, with his two dog, Ty and Stich. Blake continues to make up stories about things like space aliens and superheroes, and he has written more than 100 chapter books and graphic novels for children.

FERN CANO

Fernando Cano is an illustrator born in Mexico City, Mexico. He currently resides in Monterrey, Mexico, where he works as a free-lance illustrator and concept artist. He has done illustration work for Marvel, DC Comics, and worked on various video game projects in diverse titles. When he's not making art for comics or books, he enjoys hanging out with friends, singing, rowing, and drawing.

GLOSSARY

agile (AJ-ahyl) — able to move quickly and easily

competitor (kuhm-PE-tuh-tuhr) — a person who is trying to win in a sport or game

mud flaps (muhd flahps) — pieces of material hanging behind the tire that are designed to prevent things on the r oad from hitting the inside

nimble (NIM-buhl) — quick and light movement

outsmart (out-SMART) — to be cleverer than someone else

rubble (RUHB-uhl) — broken bricks, concrete, glass, metal, or other debris left from somethingthat has fallen down or been demolished

shudder (SHUHD-ur) — to shake from cold or fear

MORE MONSTER MYTHS

ONLY FROM

CAPSTONE